ISBN: 978-0-578-82447-5 (Print)
978-0-578-82451-2 (Ebook)

For my little brother, Arjun.
-With love.

true colors

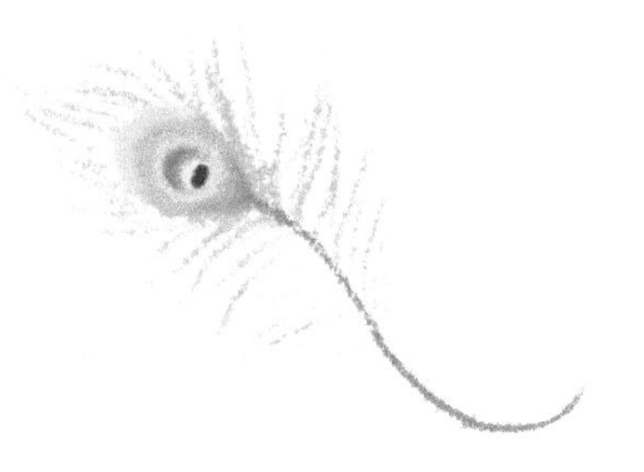

Written by: Aditi Nair
Illustrated by: Morgan Colonna

Chapter One:

Long, long ago, a peahen named Crystal lived in the vast lands of Africa. Her best friend was Alejandro, a beautiful peacock. One fine morning, Crystal looked down from her home and caught a glimpse of Alejandro with his long plumes fanned out in vibrant blues and greens.

He was showing off his beautiful feathers to all his friends. Crystal took a quick peek at her tail feathers and sighed with disappointment. *Hmph*! She wished that she could have beautiful feathers like Alejandro.

While Crystal was getting ready for the day, she stumbled upon some old maps and books. She noticed a map that could take her to Lori, the magical green elephant. Crystal decided that she was going to find Lori and seek help to change her feathers.

Crystal waved goodbye to her family and friends,

as she embarked on her journey to find Lori.

As Crystal started her journey, she was surprised to see the desert at a standstill. She had hoped for something magical to happen. *Finally!* In the distance, she could see a huge dune.

On the hike up the dune, shamrock green leaves and neon flowers suddenly surrounded her. To her amazement, with every step, the barren desert was transforming into a lush green forest!

Crystal looked around the beautiful forest in awe. As she made her way through the woods, she suddenly came across three paths-all equally inviting! She saw many forest creatures and butterflies fly into the middle path, but none through the one on the left or right. Crystal looked at the middle trail and then at her map. It did not explain anything! She decided to follow the butterflies into the middle path, hoping to find Lori.

As Crystal climbed up the mountain, it started to snow. She stopped and looked around.

Where are all the beautiful flowers? She thought as she continued along the mysterious path.

Chapter Two:

The snow had started to overlap, making the trail invisible. Crystal continued to trudge through the snow. *It would have to be at least two feet of snow!* Crystal thought as she continued forward. The bright, yellow sun embraced the white snow, making it glisten and reflect a velvety sheen around her. The intricate designs on each snowflake made Crystal wonder: *did the snowflakes feel like outsiders too? Each one is unique and beautiful in its own way. Nonetheless, did one snowflake ever want to be like the other?*

Just then, she saw two eyes watching her.

It was an arctic fox with soft, light orange paws.

“Why hello there! My name is Billy,” the fox shouted as he stood up – on all fours – to introduce himself.

“Hi Billy, my name is Crystal, and I am looking for Lori, the green elephant,” Crystal replied.

“It’s a pleasure to meet you, Crystal, but why do you seek Lori?” questioned Billy.

“All my life, I wanted to look beautiful, just like my friend Alejandro. I am looking for Lori because I want new feathers, and I want to become more confident,” Crystal replied.

“Crystal, every animal is different. It makes no sense to become what you are not,” Billy said. “When I was young, I went out to find Lori myself.”

“Billy! You are very handsome,” Crystal broke in.

“Thank you, Crystal! But, that was not how I pictured myself until I met Lori. I understood that it is okay to be different,” Billy said, looking up at the sky.

"For example, do you see those two birds? They look different in one way or the other, but they aren't disappointed," Billy said.

"Wow, I never thought of it that way," Crystal replied, looking back at her feathers. "Thank you, Billy. I will remember what you taught me," Crystal announced.

Crystal smiled at Billy as she advanced on the semi-visible trail keeping Billy's lesson in mind. After a while, it stopped snowing. There were no more snowflakes around, and the snow had started to melt. Within minutes, the trail was in sight.

Chapter Three:

Crystal stopped walking and looked around. Beautiful flowers and banana trees surrounded her!

She was enjoying the weather and strolling through the forest. Just then, *SSSPLOPPP!* Crystal slipped on a banana peel! She was like an angry bee. Annoyed, Crystal rose from the moist ground to find a long trail of banana peels. *Who could be so careless and forget to pick up their banana peels?* Crystal pondered as she looked around.

Finally, she reached the end of the trail to find a blue-faced monkey hanging from a banana tree.

"Well, hello! My name is Crystal. Are you the very careless monkey who dropped all those banana peels?" interrogated Crystal.

"Oh, um... that is probably me. I seem never to have the energy to pick up after myself," replied the monkey with a smirk.

"I forgive you; what is your name?" asked Crystal.

"My name is Joe. Are you on an adventure of some sort?" asked Joe.

"Yes. I am trying to find Lori because I want new feathers, and I want to be more confident," Crystal replied.

"Well... young child, you should be happy with what you have. When I was young, I disliked my blue face; I thought it was frightful and different, but I was wrong. I should've been as happy as I am now with my blue face and golden hair," stated Joe.

"Hmmm, maybe I should consider my feathers the way you consider your face," Crystal replied.

"Thank you, Joe, and goodbye! I hope to see you soon. Your lesson will be with me forever!" Crystal announced as she continued her journey.

Joe smiled and waved goodbye.

Chapter Four:

As Crystal was hiking Mount Green, she noticed that she was nearing her destination. Billy and Joe taught her lessons that she wasn't going to forget. She had already started to appreciate herself.

Crystal noticed that she had walked into yet another forest! The yellow-green grass expanse, with lonesome trees that dotted the horizon, amazed Crystal. There were a lot of animals, and it seemed like a safari! It was not long before that the hushed chatter of squirrels drew her attention.

As she followed the voices, all of a sudden, Crystal spotted a Siberian tiger resting under a gigantic old banyan tree!

"Hello there! My name is Russia. What is yours?" asked the tiger.

"M-m-my name is Crystal, and I am going to see Lori," stammered Crystal.

"Don't worry. I already had my lunch! Why do you seek Lori?" asked Russia.

"I want new feathers, and I want to become more confident," Crystal replied.

"What a coincidence! I wanted to see Lori and become more confident, too!" Russia said as she stood up.

"Did she help you?" asked Crystal.

"Yes, she did. She also taught me a vital lesson: the inner strength in oneself makes one confident," Russia said. " You just have to believe in yourself!" added Russia.

"Really? Maybe I just have to start believing in myself and identify my true colors!" exclaimed Crystal.

"Yes! Well, you should be on your way. It is getting dark, and Lori doesn't like to see people past midnight!" warned Russia.

"Oh! Thank you, Russia, and goodbye," waved Crystal as she paced up the mountain. Crystal was determined to reach Lori before the night sky fell.

Finally, she reached the top of Mount Green.

CRRRACK! Alarmed, Crystal looked down to find a twig that had just snapped! The dirt path rumbled and shook as Crystal bounced away from the twig. The ground transformed into a smooth cobblestone path! Awestruck, Crystal looked around, then cautiously stepped forward.

BZZZZZ! The vibration caused by the colorful ripples almost made her lose balance. She was mesmerized by the beautiful rainbow waves around her foot. As she lifted her foot off the ground, the vibration stopped, and the waves disappeared. She confidently trod across the path.

Chapter Five

The splendor and glory of a shiny platinum castle stood tall before Crystal. As Crystal entered the castle, she looked around to find Lori. Grand chandeliers hung from the ceiling, and platinum walls surrounded the throne room. Her eyes met a tall mirror that stood next to the magnificent throne.

"Hello, young one, the mirror you see is a magical one indeed," assured a voice that appeared to come from the throne. As Crystal turned around, her eyes met a magical green elephant, majestically embracing the grand throne.

The green elephant is Lori! Thought Crystal.

"The reflection cast on the mirror is what you think of yourself. What do you see, Crystal?" Lori asked.

"I see a beautiful peahen, even prettier than my friend Alejandro; her feathers shine bright," Crystal replied.

"Well done, young one! Now tell me, what brings you here?" asked Lori.

"I wanted new feathers, and I wanted to become more confident..." Crystal paused for a moment and then continued with a grin on her face, "on my journey to meet you, I made some friends who taught me that I am already beautiful. All I needed was self-appreciation!"

"I am happy that you have met my friends Billy, Joe, and Russia. I am also glad that they have helped you understand that you have always been your kind of beautiful," Lori said, then vanished into thin air with the whole castle.

Crystal looked around and was surprised to see the castle disappear! As she started her journey back home, Crystal looked at her feathers, and she felt beautiful!

She realized that this journey helped her understand the importance of self-appreciation and belief in oneself. Crystal confidently flaunted her feathers as she climbed down the mountain.

Once Crystal reached her house, she was excited to share her life-changing experiences on Mount Green. Her parents were very proud to see their young peahen grow to appreciate her true identity—her true colors.